HAPPY BEAR™, CHRISTMAS STAR

A Random House PICTUREBACK®

HAPPY BEAR,
CHRISTMAS STAR

By Jane E. Gerver
Illustrated by Bobbi Barto

Random House New York

Happy Bear slipped down in his chair, as low as he could go without falling onto the floor. *Please don't call my name*, he thought. He sneaked a peek at his teacher, Ms. Raccoon.

Uh, oh. Big mistake! "Why, Happy," said Ms. Raccoon. "I didn't give *you* a part in the Winter Pageant. Now, let's see…how about playing the part of Jack Frost? That should be a lot of fun!"

The teacher looked around the room. "Start studying your lines, everybody. Remember, the pageant is in a few days, just before Christmas."

After school Ms. Raccoon had all the actors read their lines out loud.

"I am Snowflake, the fairy who covers everything in a blanket of white," said Daisy Bunny.

"I am Old Man Winter, the fellow who brings cold winds," said Squeaky Squirrel.

"I am Jack Frost," said Happy. "I...I...um...I zip—"

"No, no, Happy," Ms. Raccoon said gently. "I *nip* at people's noses."

Squeaky Squirrel laughed. "Zip at people's noses!" he said. "What does Happy think he is—a *zipper*?"

"That Squeaky is a real nut," Happy grumbled to his friend Busy Bunny as they walked home from school.

"Well, he might be nutty, but he has a good memory," Busy said. "He has more lines than anyone else."

"I have a good memory too," said Happy. "Just not when I'm nervous," he added to himself.

Happy decided to practice his lines until he knew them backward and forward.

He rehearsed with Busy and Daisy.

He rehearsed with Mommy and Daddy.

He even rehearsed with his little sister, Lily. She couldn't really read, but she was a great audience of one. And she knew just when to clap.

"Hey, Happy!" called Squeaky Squirrel. He popped his head around the side of the house. "Bet you won't remember your lines in front of a *real* audience," he said with a smirk.

In spite of Squeaky's teasing, Happy felt very pleased. He knew his lines, all of them. Maybe he would be a star—a Christmas star in the Winter Pageant! He fell asleep the night before the play and dreamed of being a hit.

THE
WINTER
PAGEANT

Happy woke up the next morning still feeling very pleased. He jumped out of bed and looked in the mirror.

"I am Jack Frost—" he tried to say. But no words came out. Not one! He had used his voice rehearsing so much that now it had disappeared.

This was terrible. Tonight was the pageant. How could Happy be in a play if he didn't have a voice?

Happy didn't try to say anything to anyone. He kept busy so he wouldn't have to talk. If he gave it a rest, maybe his voice would come back.

He read the funnies in the newspaper.

He went to Pawprint Pond to watch the ice skaters.

He even cleaned up his room, including under the bed.

Finally evening arrived. Happy changed into his costume backstage. Everyone was excited. Everyone was chattering—except for Happy.

It was almost showtime. Happy peeked out from behind the stage curtain. He could see Mommy, Daddy, and Lily in the audience.

"Come on, voice. Come on, voice," Happy croaked softly. "You've had your rest."

"Places, everyone!" said Ms. Raccoon.

The curtain opened, and the Winter Pageant began.

"I am Snowflake, the fairy who covers everything in a blanket of white," said Daisy.

"I am Old Man Winter, the fellow who brings cold winds," said Squeaky.

Happy took a deep breath. "I am Jack Frost," he began hoarsely.

Squeaky giggled. "Jack Frost with a sore throat," the squirrel whispered teasingly.

Happy looked over at Squeaky and frowned. And then suddenly he smiled.

A sore throat! What a good idea. Why couldn't Happy pretend to be Jack Frost with a sore throat? People got sore throats all the time in the winter.

Happy turned and faced the audience again.

"I am Jack Frost," Happy croaked. "Usually, I nip at people's noses and cover windowpanes with ice. But tonight I have a sore throat. I got it from—from the flu fairy, who brings colds and coughs to children everywhere in wintertime."

The audience laughed and laughed and clapped and clapped. They made enough noise to drown out Squeaky, who was whining, "That wasn't in the script, Ms. Raccoon!"

At the end of the pageant the curtain closed. Happy could hear the audience applauding. Then the curtain opened again, and all the players bowed.

"Bravo, Happy! Bravo!" shouted Happy's family.

Happy Bear beamed. He really was a Christmas star, after all!